18140

Phoebe and the Spelling Bee

Hyperion Books for Children
New York

HYPERION BOOKS FOR CHILDREN
Text and illustrations © 1996 by Barney Saltzberg.
All rights reserved.

For information address Hyperion Books for Children, 114 Fifth Avenue,
New York, New York 10011-5690.

Printed in Hong Kong by South China Printing Company (1988) Ltd.

First published in 1996 by Hyperion Books for Children.
1 3 5 7 9 10 8 6 4 2

Nestlé is a registered trademark of Nestlé USA, Inc.

The artwork for each picture is prepared using ink and color wash.

This book is set in 17-point American Typewriter.

Library of Congress Cataloging-in-Publication Data
Saltzberg, Barney
Phoebe and the spelling bee / Barney Saltzberg—1st ed.
p. cm.
Summary: Participating in her class spelling bee, Phoebe uses her
wonderful imagination to remember tough word spellings.
ISBN 0-7868-0140-9 (trade)—ISBN 0-7868-2114-0 (lib. bdg.)
[1. English language—Spelling—Fiction. 2. Imagination—Fiction.
3. Memory—Fiction.] I. Title
PZ7.S65933Ww 1995
[Fic]—dc20 94-37547

"Friday we will have our first spelling bee," announced Ms. Ravioli. "Here's a list of words you should know."

I slid down in my chair. "I'm going to be sick on Friday," I whispered to Katie.

"Don't be silly, Phoebe," said Katie. "Spelling is easy."

"I'm allergic to spelling," I told her.

"I'll help you," said Katie.

We ate lunch together. Katie looked over the spelling list. "This will be a breeze!" she said.

I drew dots all over my arm and started groaning, "Oooohhhh!"

"What's the matter?" asked Katie.

"I think I've got chicken pox!" I said.

"Spell **actor**," said Katie.

"**A-k-d-o-r**," I said.

"That's what it sounds like," said Katie, "but it's spelled differently."

She showed me the word on the spelling list. I saw that you could break the word into two parts—**act** and **or**.

"If I could **act or** spell, I'd **act**!" I said. "**A-c-t-o-r!**"

"That's right!" said Katie.

"Try spelling **brontosaurus**," said Katie.

I dropped to the ground, holding my leg. "Oh, it's broken!" I cried. "A **brontosaurus** knocked me over, and I broke my leg!"

"I'm waiting!" said Katie.
 "Race you to class backward," I shouted,
and then I ran inside.

That night
Katie called me
to find out how
I was doing
with my spelling list.

"Great!" I said.

I was folding
the spelling list
into a paper
airplane.

The next morning Ms. Ravioli asked how many
students had been studying for the spelling bee.
Everyone raised their hand. Except me.
I was under the table, studying my shoes.

"Phoebe," said Ms. Ravioli, "have you looked at your spelling list?"

I sat up in my chair. "Once there was an **actor** who played a **brontosaurus**."

Everybody laughed. I sank in my chair.

"Settle down, class," said Ms. Ravioli. "It sounds like Phoebe has an unusual way of learning her words."

I looked at Katie's spelling list on our way home.
"Try spelling **graceful**," she said.
"The **actor** who played a **brontosaurus** was
graceful!" I said.

"You're great at making up stories," said Katie.
"But the spelling bee is in three days!"

"I know," I said. Then I ran to get some ice cream.

I knew I had better study or I would really embarrass myself at the spelling bee.

I found my spelling list on my bedroom floor, still folded into an airplane.

"If I can fly this into the trash can on the first try," I thought, "I'll be the winner of the spelling bee."

The plane flew under a chair. "That was just a warm-up."

The plane flew into the wall. "Didn't count."

I stood on a chair
and dropped the airplane
into the trash. "Yes!"

I had a victory celebration
and danced around my room.

Then my father told me
it was time to go to bed.

The next morning Ms. Ravioli said we would have a mock spelling bee.

I decided it was time to get sick.

"Ooooh!" I moaned.

"What seems to be the problem?" asked Ms. Ravioli.

"I ate too many pieces of pizza with pineapple last night," I said. "I feel sick."

"I think a visit to the nurse's office would be a good idea," said Ms. Ravioli.

"You haven't studied at all, have you?" whispered Katie.

"Yes I have!" I said.

I dragged my feet to the
nurse's office. Now my stomach
really did feel awful.
I had never lied to Katie before.

When I got back from the nurse's office, Katie handed me a note. It said:

YOU DIDN'T STUDY AND YOU DIDN'T HAVE A STOMACHACHE AND REAL FRIENDS TELL EACH OTHER THE TRUTH!

I didn't speak to Katie for the rest of the day.

That night I felt terrible. I hadn't been honest with my best friend, and I wasn't ready for the spelling bee.

I looked at my spelling list.

The first word I learned was **method**. I thought of a caveman saying his name, "**Me, Thod**."

I learned **telephone** by thinking of a phone, which you *tell* your friends things on.
The second **l** in *tell* becomes an **e**.

I even learned how to spell **consonant**. It was easy because I figured there were three parts, **con**, **son**, and **ant**.

The next day was Friday. Spelling bee day.

I brought Katie a tulip and said I was sorry for having lied.

Ms. Ravioli explained the rules. I could feel my heart beating fast. What if I looked stupid in front of the whole class?

I started to raise my hand to go to the nurse's office. I decided to have the flu.

Katie wished me good luck. I was happy she was still talking to me. I put down my hand.

I decided not to have the flu after all.

18140

During the spelling bee, Sheldon couldn't spell **disaster**. So he had to sit down.

When Jorge couldn't spell **telephone** correctly, he asked to go to the bathroom.

Marcia almost remembered how to spell **consonant**, but she forgot one of the **n**s.

I had to spell **Wednesday**. I knew the word had
three parts, all with three letters.

I thought of a wedding day where chocolate
chips were thrown instead of rice. **Wed** for wedding, **nes** for Nestlé chocolate, and **day**!

I spelled the word, "**W-e-d-n-e-s-d-a-y**."

"Nice job!" said Ms. Ravioli.

Katie spelled her word perfectly.
"**N-a-t-u-r-a-l**,"
she said.

After a while there were only three of us still spelling, and then came **brontosaurus**. I tried sounding it out, "**b-r-a-w-n-t-o-e-s-o-r-u-s**."

"That was a good try," said Ms. Ravioli, "but it's not the correct spelling."

"The **actor** was a **natural** and very **graceful**," I said. The whole class was staring at me.

"The **a-c-t-o-r** played a **brontosaurus** and met a caveman who said, '**Me, Thod**,' which is how you break down the spelling of **method**. Thod asked the dinosaur if he had heard about the volcano **disaster**. The dinosaur said no, but he wondered if Thod knew what a **c-o-n-s-o-n-a-n-t** was."

I looked at Ms. Ravioli.

"Please continue," she said.

So I did. "Thod and the dinosaur heard a **t-e-l-e-p-h-o-n-e** ringing in a tree!"

Katie smiled.

"The call was for a **p-e-d-e-s-t-r-i-a-n** who was jogging by, eating a piece of **c-h-o-c-o-l-a-t-e**." I told my class that a great way to remember how to spell **chocolate** is to think of someone named *Choco*, who's *late*.

"When Choco saw the **brontosaurus**, he screamed and ran the other way! The caveman and the dinosaur fell on the ground and laughed!

"That's the **l-e-g-e-n-d** of Thod and the brontosaurus. You can remember how to spell **legend** by thinking of your **leg** and **end**!"

Everybody clapped when I finished. Even though I couldn't spell **brontosaurus**, I had used up all the words on my list to tell a story. Charlie couldn't spell **brontosaurus** either—but Katie could, so she won the spelling bee. She was great!

Ms. Ravioli gave Katie a certificate that said
CHAMPION SPELLER.

I got a certificate, too, only mine said
WONDERFUL IMAGINATION!